3.9

Witho

D0577002

COOPÉRATIVE MARAICHÈRE DU HAVR

85 - St HILAIRE DE RIEZ   Tél. 24 NO

PoiRe	PeAR
LAit	milk
BonBon	Candy
PAin	BRead
oeuf	Egg
BeURre	Butter
Jus De pomme	Appel juice
Sel	SALT
SAVON	SoaP
FromAge	cheeSe
Vin	WinE
conCombre	cucumBer
thon	tuna
gateau	Cake

To Chloë and Pia

Atheneum Books for Young Readers
An imprint of Simon & Schuster Children's
Publishing Division
1230 Avenue of the Americas, New York,
New York 10020
Copyright © 2004 by Giselle Potter

All rights reserved, including the right of
reproduction in whole or in part in any form.

Book design by Ann Bobco
The text for this book is set in Gararond.
The illustrations for this book are rendered in
pencil, ink, gouache, gesso, and watercolor.
Manufactured in China
First Edition
10 9 8 7 6 5 4 3 2 1
Library of Congress Cataloging-in-Publication Data
Potter, Giselle.
Chloë's birthday . . . and me / Giselle Potter.
p. cm.
"An Anne Schwartz Book."
Sequel to: The year I didn't go to school.
Summary: When attention must be paid to her
little sister Chloë's birthday, Giselle, who lives
with her family in France, makes inappropriate
gift suggestions and almost spoils the big day.
ISBN 0-689-86230-X
[1. Sisters—Fiction. 2. Birthdays—Fiction.
3. Gifts—Fiction. 4. France—Fiction.] I. Title.
PZ7.P8519Ch 2004
[E]—dc21
2002038524

Chloë's

Potter, Giselle.
Chlok's birthday--and
me /
c2004.
33305209026727
ca   06/17/05

Birthday... and Me

By
Giselle
Potter

An Anne Schwartz Book
Atheneum Books for Young Readers
New York   London   Toronto   Sydney   Singapore

SANTA CLARA COUNTY LIBRARY

. 3 3305 20902 6727

"It's almost Chloë's birthday,"

my mom whispered in my ear as we picked
blackberries. "Let's go to town and find a present."

It was the summer my sister turned five, and we were in France, staying in a little stone house on Madame Bianchini's guinea-hen farm. There were millions of blackberry bushes everywhere and we picked and ate them until our mouths were stained dark purple. Chloë was putting every one of her berries straight into her little purple mouth with her little purple hands.

As we drove into Le Cerisier—which means "the cherry tree" in French—I squeezed my eyes shut. *I wish it were* my *birthday, I wish it were* my *birthday,* I said in my head over and over. Chloë was too little to even care that it was her birthday, and my birthday was my favorite day of the year—much better than Christmas or Halloween because all the attention is just for you.

In the town market I pulled at the lacy socks hanging from strings.
"Too big for her," Mom said. Maybe so, but they looked exactly my size.

I pointed to the chocolates and candies in the store window. "Too
sugary," said Mom. Oh, well. If we'd bought her candy, I could have
definitely eaten some.

Then we saw it. There, in the window of Madame Fifi's
parfumerie, was a little round bottle of perfume called . . . Chloë!
It sparkled as if it wanted us to notice it.

"Look, G, it's been waiting for us!" Mom giggled with excitement.
Inside, the store smelled so sweet and spicy my nose tingled with an
about-to-sneeze feeling.

"Ahhh *oui*, Chloëee!" the pretty saleswoman exclaimed
when we pointed at the bottle. Her shiny red fingernails took
it off the shelf and wrapped it up in gold paper and ribbons.
"Is there a perfume called Giselle?" I asked as we left, but
no one seemed to hear me.

I was proud to hold the *parfumerie* bag and pretend it was mine as I swung it back and forth through town.

"Don't show this to Chloë," Mom reminded me. "It's a surprise."

"Can I get some red nails like that lady's?" I asked.

"Maybe when it's your birthday." But my birthday was almost a whole year away.

The next morning, the guinea hens screeched like old women, and I collected all the polka-dotted feathers they left in a trail behind them. Dad made a beautiful finger puppet that looked like a bird, and we glued all the feathers to it. I put it on my finger, wiggled it around, and squawked. "*My* birthday, *my* birthday, *my* birthday!" I made the puppet say.

My dad's eyebrows rose into his forehead, making thousands of little lines. "You know this is for Chloë," he said.

I squawked louder.

On the morning of Chloë's birthday, it already seemed like it had been her birthday for about a week. Mom woke me up early and we made a garland of dandelions. I drew a card with a picture of Chloë and me as princesses, while Chloë slept later and later.

"Happy birthday, babe!" my mom cried when she
finally woke up. Dad placed the garland on her messy
hair. "I dub you Queen Chloë," he said.

I reminded myself that Chloë was really just a baby.

We packed blankets and bathing suits, presents and ourselves into our little car and headed off to the beach. When Chloë crossed to my side of the backseat, I didn't pinch her since it was her birthday.

We stopped at La Belle Pâtisserie to pick out a chocolate cake, and had "Chloë" written on top with white sugar that looked like toothpaste.

"I'm going to eat your name off the cake," I told Chloë.

"No!" She stomped her foot.

"Come on, girls, we'll all eat some cake later . . . especially the birthday girl," Mom said, walking over to smooth Chloë's hair.

At the beach there were little striped tents to change
in and some other families wearing much smaller bathing
suits than we were. While Chloë and my dad ran to the
water, I came up with a good idea. What if I hid Chloë's
perfume in the sand, and she could try to find it?

That would be a fun game, and there was
only a teeny chance it would get lost. As Mom
put candles in the cake, I dug a hole near our
blanket and stuck her fancy gold box in it.

I padded and smoothed the sand, then ran screaming
"Ahhhh!" into the water with my arms spread out.
Chloë was riding on Dad's shoulders, and I jumped on
his back so that we all became a giant, floating whale.

It was hard keeping sand off the cake, and our "Happy Birthday" song got lost in the wind, but Chloë didn't even notice. Dad gave her the guinea-hen puppet and she moved it around like a fish instead of a hen and made peeping sounds instead of squawks.

"Your other present is very nearby, but you'll have to find it," I told Chloë. I smiled smartly at my parents.

"HOT . . . COLD . . .
VERY COLD . . . WARM!"
I shouted as Chloë crawled around the sand like a crab.
My parents looked worried, waiting for my clues.
"HOT! HOT! HOT!" I yelled as she dug at the very spot I
remembered, her missing-teeth smile wide and her eyes glittering.
As she dug, I started to get a bad feeling. Now Dad was
digging . . . and Mom was digging too. My ears started buzzing.
My throat felt hard as I swallowed. I started digging.
"Can't you remember where you buried it, Giselle?" Dad asked.
I just shook my head slowly because I couldn't talk.

Mom and Dad shot each other looks while Chloë and I kept digging.
Chloë didn't seem upset yet, but I could tell it wouldn't be long.

"Maybe we can smell where it is," I suggested. Mom looked furious,
so I quickly got on all fours and pretended to be an excited dog. Chloë
copied me, sniffing and barking. Faster and faster we sniffed, until it
seemed like Chloë had forgotten all about presents and birthdays.
Finally we flopped over and stared
at the sky.

"You can bury me if you want," I told Chloë, and she covered me all up, except for right around my face. She made my hands and feet look like monster hands and feet and then she buried herself.

"I'm coming to get you!"
I monster-roared, and wiggled
my arms and legs until they
popped out.

Chloë made a little yelp.
She squirmed and dug herself
deeper . . . and then . . .

"There's something under . . . *look!*"
she cried. Her hand emerged from the
sand holding the little gold box.

"You found it!" Mom said when Chloë
brought it to show her.

"Yippee, Chloë!" Dad shouted.
"Hooray for Chloë, hooray for Chloë!"
I sang, skipping in circles around her.

Chloë ripped the fancy paper and ribbon apart, pulled out the little bottle, and stared at it.

"It's a perfume called Chloë!" my mom said, pointing to the label. "Giselle and I picked it out for you."

Chloë stared some more. But then slowly her big eyes looked up at me. They glowed like full moons. "It's named after me," she said in wonder.

"Happy birthday, Chlo," I said in our secret funny voice, and she sprayed a big puff of perfume right in her face and then in mine.

14 Jun 1974 at Ham
I will act uery nice
and I will not
make my mommy
Bad.

I Think Alice was Quite BRave
in Wonderland

02

JARDIN DU LUXEMBOURG
PARC DE JEUX
LES PETITS POUSSINS

UNE ENTRÉE